*min**e**dition*

North American edition published 2019 by Michael Neugebauer Publishing Ltd. Hong Kong

Michael Neugebauer Publishing Ltd.,
Unit 28, 5/F, Metro Centre, Phase 2, No.21 Lam Hing Street, Kowloon Bay, Kowloon, Hong Kong
Phone: +852 2807 1711, e-mail: info@minedition.com
This book was printed in December 2018 at L.Rex Ltd
3/F., Blue Box Factory Building, 25 Hing Wo Street, Tin Wan, Aberdeen, Hong Kong, China
Typesetting in Candara
Library of Congress Cataloging-in-Publication Data available upon request.

ISBN 978-988-8341-83-2
10 9 8 7 6 5 4 3 2 1
First Impression

For more information please visit our website: www.minedition.com

MANNY LOSES HIS FANGS

Giuliano Ferri

minedition

Manny the vampire bat was the terror of everyone he met.

He loved to scare the other animals. Whenever he'd show his sharp fangs they would flee! He found it so delightful.

Manny hoped that with enough practice he could become the scariest vampire bat in the world.

But one day while biting into an apple, one of his frightening fangs fell out. "What's this?" Manny wondered.

The next day his other fang fell out, too. "Oh no," Manny thought. "Without my fangs I won't be able to scare any of the animals anymore!"

Now Manny knew he could never become the scariest vampire bat in the world.

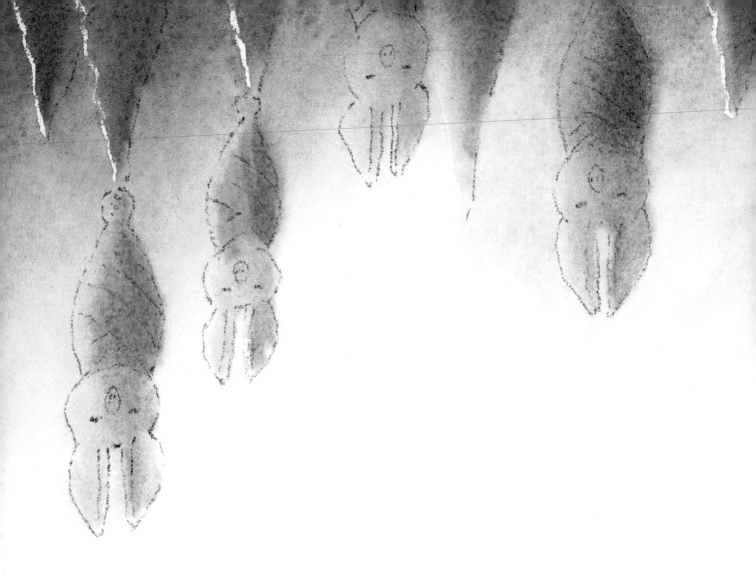

Sad and discouraged, he returned to his cave.

His grandfather tried to reassure him. "Those were your baby fangs," he told Manny. "Your big fangs will grow in soon." But Manny decided it was hopeless. His scaring days were over, he thought, and he was never going to leave this cave again!

One day while he was asleep,
something flew into the cave
and smacked Manny awake.

It was someone's ball.

Annoyed, Manny gave the ball
a tremendous kick, and it sailed
high up out of the cave.

From outside he heard a gasp and the sound of applause.

Peeking outside his cave, Manny saw a group of players
who eyed him with admiration.
"Do you want to play with us?" the cat asked.

Manny sulked.
They were not at all afraid of him.

Still, Manny had liked the sound of that applause, so he decided to give it a try.

After a few days of practice he started to get really good, and he liked how much his new friends wanted to be around him.

"Maybe it's okay not being the scariest vampire bat in the world," he thought.

A few weeks later, Manny realized that what his grandfather had told him was true: his big fangs really were starting to grow in. Now he was sad for a new reason—he knew everyone would be afraid of him again, and he wouldn't be able to play with his new friends anymore.

Once again he decided to hide away up in his cave.

But the sound of loud voices outside woke him.
A group of bullies had decided to take his friends'
ball, and they weren't going to give it back.

Manny was angry, and he decided to spring into action. He flew up, showed his fangs and let out the loudest screech the animals had ever heard.

The bullies instantly dropped the ball and took off as fast as their trotters could carry them.

"Well," Manny said to the others, "you probably won't want such a scary vampire bat around you anymore."
But to his surprise his new friends hugged him and thanked him for saving their ball.
"Of course you can play with us," the mouse said.
"Just because you're scary to others doesn't mean you're scary to us. Friends are friends no matter how they look."

Manny felt happier than he ever had before.